HOL/CH

Please return / renew by date shown.
You can renew it at:
norlink.norfolk.gov.uk
or by telephone: 0344 800 8006
Please have your library card & PIN ready

NORFOLK LIBRARY
AND INFORMATION SERVICE

WITH THANKS TO STELLA, STEVE, AMY AND TOBY JELLISS FOR HAVING THE FORESIGHT TO TAKE A KENYAN HOLIDAY EIGHT YEARS AGO.

FOR THE INTERNATIONAL ELEPHANT FOUNDATION - JB & SV

STRIPES PUBLISHING
An imprint of Magi Publications
1 The Coda Centre, 189 Munster Road,
London SW6 6AW

A paperback original
First published in Great Britain in 2010

ISBN: 978-1-84715-115-5

A CIP catalogue record for this book is available from the British Library.

Printed and bound in the UK.

10 9 8 7 6 5 4 3 2 1

WILD RESCUE

SAFARI SURVIVAL

J. Burchett and S. Vogler

STATUS: FILE CLOSED
LOCATION
ALASKA, USA
CODENAME SNOW WHITE

STATUS: FILE CLOSED
LOCATION:
SICHUAN, CHINA
CODE NAME: JING JING

STATUS: FILE CLOSED
LOCATION:
SOUTH BORNEO
CODE NAME: KAWAN

STATUS: FILE CLOSED
LOCATION:
SUMATRA, INDONESIA
CODE NAME: TORA

STATUS: LIVE
LOCATION:
KENYA, AFRICA
CODE NAME: TOMBOI

RESCUE
MISSION DATABASE

CHAPTER ONE

"Take cover," Ben hissed. "There's someone coming."

His twin sister Zoe tried to dive aside, but it was too late. A shadowy figure, face hidden by a black mask, stepped out in front of her in the dark and held up its gun.

Zap! With horror, Zoe saw a flash on her chest. She'd been hit.

The stranger whipped off her mask and grinned.

"Erika!" exclaimed Zoe. "What are you doing at Lasertrail?"

"Trailing you two." Erika grinned and turned off her gun. "Your godfather sent me. Wild has a new mission for you."

"Cool!" gasped Ben. "So we're off to Wild HQ for our briefing, are we?"

"No time for that," said Erika, guiding them to the exit. "We're going straight to Africa. My car's outside to take us to the plane. I've told your gran about your mission so she won't be expecting you home today."

Ben and Zoe looked at each other in excitement. Ever since their eccentric godfather, Dr Stephen Fisher, had recruited them into Wild, they'd found themselves being whizzed all over the world. Not many eleven-year-olds could say they were operatives for a top secret organization dedicated to saving animals in danger.

Their parents were vets who were currently working abroad. They thought

Ben and Zoe were safe at home enjoying their summer holiday with their grandmother, and had no idea their children travelled the world saving animals, just like their mum and dad!

"This must be a *really* urgent mission," said Ben, as they sped along a deserted country lane. "What's it all about?"

"You'll find out once we're airborne," Erika said. "You know Dr Fisher likes to explain things himself."

A small airstrip came into view. Erika drove the car straight into a battered barn, where an ordinary-looking private jet was waiting. They scrambled aboard and Erika began the pre-flight checks.

"I'm glad Uncle Stephen's made the plane out of recycled stuff," said Zoe, holding her nose as the engine fired up, "but I wish the fuel wasn't chicken poo and egg yolks. I'll never get used to the smell."

They soared into the sky and were soon out over the sea.

"What's our mission then?" asked Ben.

Erika flicked a switch.

A shimmering hologram appeared in the air. It was their godfather, his usual straw hat perched on top of his spiky red hair.

"Greetings, godchildren," he said. "If you press the red button on the console in front of you, you'll find a clue to your task. And it's a big clue. Get in touch when you've worked out which animal it comes from."

And with that the hologram disappeared.

Zoe pressed the button and a small compartment opened up to reveal a glass eyeball.

Ben and Zoe studied it.

The iris was golden brown with a round black pupil.

"Uncle Stephen said it was a big clue," said Zoe, puzzled, "but this isn't an

enormous eyeball. I wonder what he meant.
Let's think… Africa."

"Lion, leopard, wildebeest," muttered
Ben, turning the eye over in his hand.
"Wait a minute. It's simple. He means the
biggest animal." He flicked a switch next to
the speaker that connected to Wild HQ.
"Are you there, Uncle Stephen?"

"Receiving you loud and clear," replied Dr Fisher. "Have you cracked the puzzle already?"

"It's an elephant," said Ben, triumphantly.

"Well done," came their godfather's voice. "African elephant. They're bigger than the Indian ones and more dangerous." He sounded grave. "James, here at Wild, has picked up a tweet from a charity worker out in Kenya. There's a bull calf called Tomboi in trouble in the Samburu National Park. He has a wire snare round his leg and it could easily become infected. He and his mother are already starting to trail behind the herd."

"So our job is to find him," said Zoe.

"Absolutely," said Uncle Stephen. "Then sedate the little chap, remove the snare and give him some antibiotics. That's his only chance of recovery."

"There's a veterinary kit stowed under your seat with your backpacks," Erika told them.

Ben grabbed the small canvas bag and examined the tranquillizer guns and medication bottles inside.

"This is the sort of equipment that Mum and Dad have," he said eagerly.

"The tranquillizer guns are not just for Tomboi," Erika told them. "You must have them at the ready whenever you're out on your own. There are dangerous wild animals in Kenya."

Zoe opened her backpack.

"Sleeping bag, food rations, binoculars, night-vision goggles – and of course my BUG," she said, taking out the small gizmo that looked like a hand-held games console. "We couldn't do without these." She tapped some keys and brought up a satellite map. "Hey! This plane's super fast. We're over Italy already."

"One thing puzzles me, Uncle Stephen," Ben said. "How did the snare get round

Tomboi's leg? Surely all animals are safe on wildlife reserves – and anyway, isn't game hunting illegal in Kenya?"

"It is," came Dr Fisher's voice. "I'm afraid we've stumbled upon a rather nasty business. Someone is hunting these elephants. People in the local village are saying that several elephant carcasses have been found."

"Were the elephants shot?" asked Zoe.

"Yes," said her godfather solemnly. "And then the heads were taken and the flesh cut from the bodies. Unusually, some were only youngsters."

"Gross!" exclaimed Ben.

"That's horrific," said Zoe in disgust.

"So you see how urgent this case is," said Uncle Stephen. "We believe that, somehow, Tomboi's injury is linked to the elephant slaughter. There were signs that at least one of the dead calves had been snared too."

"Why haven't you told the authorities?" asked Zoe.

"The Kenya Wildlife Service looks after a huge area and is very overworked. It can't chase up every lead without good evidence," replied her godfather. "And so far all we have is carcasses. Of course we could tell them about Tomboi's leg and they'd have him taken to the nearest animal hospital, but they might not be able to get to him straight away; and with the hunters at large he'd still be in danger when he returned to the wild."

"Although our first priority is to sort out his leg, we've decided on a rather risky plan," Erika added. "Once you've treated Tomboi, you leave him and his mother where they are and try to find out who these hunters are."

"And try to get the evidence to put them in prison." Their godfather paused. "Are you willing to take on this dangerous mission?"

"Try and stop us!" declared Ben.

CHAPTER TWO

"We have to get to Tomboi before anything else happens to him," gasped Zoe, after Uncle Stephen had signed off.

"And find out who's behind all this," added Ben.

"Your godfather has invented a new gizmo to help you gather information," said Erika.

She took out a small case from her pocket and tossed it to Zoe. Inside was a metallic disc about the size of a drawing pin.

"It's called an OWL," Erika told them.

"The Outstanding Watching and Listening device. It's perfect for tracking any suspect. As soon as you press it on to the target it attaches itself with a blob of powerful glue. It contains a miniature camera and microphone. The images and sounds will be transmitted directly to your BUGs."

"That's amazing," said Zoe. "And it's so tiny."

"Dr Fisher wants to give you a demonstration," said Erika, tapping some keys to send a message. "Turn your BUGs to OWL mode."

Ben and Zoe scrolled through their menus to OWL and hit enter.

At once the wobbly image of a high-tech computer suite flashed up on their screens.

"That's the Control Room in Wild HQ," gasped Ben.

"Welcome to the demonstration of my Outstanding Watching and Listening device," came Uncle Stephen's voice through their BUGs. "You should be seeing what I'm seeing – the Control Room in Wild HQ transmitted by the OWL attached to my hat! It may be a bit jerky as I'm walking around."

The picture swung round to show James studying some data, then the coffee machine and Dr Fisher's desk, which was covered in a jumble of papers, wires and bits of metal.

"Messy as ever!" said Ben. "I wonder what he's inventing now?"

"I expect you're wondering what I'm inventing now," said Dr Fisher. "It's a work in progress. An automatic egg cracker which—"

There was a muffled thump and the scene lurched sideways. The children could see under the desk now, a mass of discarded sweet wrappers and pen tops.

Then the image spun to reveal their godfather's face. He'd taken off his hat and was peering into the OWL. He looked pink-cheeked and his hair was standing on end.

"Sorry about that!" He gave them a huge, beaming smile. "I tripped over my chair."

Ben grinned at Zoe. Their godfather was a brilliant man, but he won top prize for clumsiness!

"Good luck with your mission," boomed Uncle Stephen. "We'll speak soon. Over and out. Well, it will be when you switch off the OWL function."

Ben and Zoe hit the exit button.

"The OWL also sends a signal to the satellite map on your BUG screens," said Erika. "If you turn to that now…"

They did as she said and a world map appeared. A tiny red light was pulsing over the North Sea. When they zoomed in they saw it was pinpointed on Wild Island.

"So it's a tracker too," said Zoe, impressed.

"I'm going to find out all I can about the Samburu National Park," said Ben, turning to the onboard computer and logging on to the internet. "It's near the foothills of Mount Kenya. The tribe who live there are also called the Samburu." He scrolled down. "It says here they keep an eye on the herd and take tourists out to see them. So we'll

be able to find out where Tomboi is. And
we might pick up some info on the dead
elephants." He brought up another website
and was soon engrossed in the information.
"Elephants live to about seventy... Females
and young live in herds..."

"He's safely on Planet Research!" Zoe
said, turning to Erika. "Who do you think's
doing this to the elephants?" she asked.
"Could it be ivory poachers?"

"I don't think so," said Erika. "They're
taking the heads, that's for sure, but ivory
poachers only take the tusks – not the flesh.
I'm wondering if we've stumbled upon some
illegal bush meat trade."

"People eat elephants?" Zoe burst out.

Erika nodded solemnly.

"But why have they targeted Tomboi?"
Zoe was puzzled. "There's not much meat
on a youngster."

"This is awful!" Ben suddenly shouted, his

eyes fixed to the screen.

Zoe felt sick when she saw the new website he was looking at – Hunting Holidays International.

Men with guns stood proudly by the bloody corpses of tigers, lions, elephants, rhino and buffalo. Adverts down the sides of the web page encouraged the reader to have their trophy animal heads mounted on the finest teak and mahogany.

"'Come face to face with nature in the raw'," read Zoe, struggling to get the words out. "'Your friends will gasp at your bravery as you outwit the fiercest animals in the world.'"

"It could be trophy hunters wanting the heads," exclaimed Ben.

Erika nodded. "It's certainly a worthwhile line of enquiry. As hunting's illegal in Kenya it couldn't be done openly. But that doesn't mean it's not happening."

Zoe clicked through the photos on the hunting site. It was hard to look at the dead animals. The hunters beamed at the cameras as if they'd done something very clever.

"The same faces keep coming up. Look at that smug bloke with cheeks like a bulldog and badges all over his hat. Frank Hall, President of the British Big Game Hunters Club. He says he's shot animals on every continent." She blinked away the sudden tears that sprang into her eyes. "I can't bear to think of that happening to little Tomboi."

Ben flicked off the monitor, making the gruesome pictures disappear. "The minute we get to Kenya we're going to start investigating. First stop – the Samburu village to find out what we can."

CHAPTER THREE

Ben and Zoe hurried across the flagstoned courtyard of the Amani Lodge. The hotel was deep in the Samburu National Park and boasted every luxury. A fountain sparkled in the bright afternoon sun and guests lounged around the swimming pool under thatched umbrellas, sipping drinks. Parrots squawked in the surrounding trees and, every now and then, black-faced monkeys darted across the floor in search of something to eat, until they were chased away by the waiters.

"It makes a change staying somewhere this posh," said Zoe, gazing around. "Look at all the rich tourists chilling out."

"We've got more important things to do," said Ben. "Get a move on. The leaflet said the village tour leaves in three minutes."

Zoe quickened her pace. "I wonder how Erika's getting on following up her lead."

They'd only just checked in at the lodge when a message had come from Wild headquarters that illegal bush meat was being sold in a town half a day's drive away. Erika had gone speeding off in a hired jeep to see if it was linked to the slaughter of the elephants.

"How could Erika be following up her lead?" said Ben in a mock questioning tone. "Our tutor's ill in bed, remember?"

"Of course!" Zoe grinned.

They had concocted this story just in case anyone asked where their guardian was.

They climbed some steps to a lawned garden. Here and there, gazelles grazed on the short cropped grass as if they were out on the plain.

"This is such a beautiful place!" Zoe went on. "It's hard to imagine that horrible things are happening to the elephants not so far away. I hope we can get some useful information from the Samburu. Where did the leaflet say the trip to the village started from?"

"Here at the north garden," said Ben. "But I can't see anyone."

A teenage boy in a green Amani Lodge uniform was weeding a flower bed.

"Excuse me," called Ben. The boy looked up and grinned. He wore a staff name badge with "Runo" on it. "Does the tour of the village leave from here?"

"Yes," said the boy. "It went two hours ago – at one o'clock."

"What?" gasped Zoe.

Ben checked his watch and looked sheepish. "Oops! I forgot to change to Kenyan time."

"But we need to get to the village as soon as possible," said Zoe, worried. The boy looked at her. "I mean, we were looking forward to going today."

Runo put down his trowel. "Can you ride a camel?" he asked, his eyes dancing with mischief.

"No," said Zoe.

"Yes!" insisted Ben.

Zoe glared at her brother. "We've never ridden camels in our lives," she hissed.

Ben shrugged. "We're good horse riders. It can't be that different."

"I can get you camels now," said Runo. "Make trip to the village very fast."

"Great!" said Ben, getting out his wallet. "How much?"

"Nothing," said the boy. "But you will take package of kitchen leftovers to my grandfather for his goats. He lives there. His name is Wambua. You follow me."

"I thought you said this would be easy," said
Zoe, gripping tightly to the front of her
camel's saddle as her mount lurched from side
to side. "It's nothing like horse riding at all."

"Just hold the reins and keep it steady,"
called Ben from his high perch. "Runo said
the camels are very well trained. They often
take tourists on rides to the village."

"I'm sure we weren't meant to take them
out without a handler," said Zoe. "When
we got to the camel compound, Runo was
very secretive."

"It nearly wasn't a secret after you let out that shriek!" said Ben.

"I thought I was going to fall off when it got up rear end first," protested Zoe.

"It's fine when you get used to it," said Ben smugly. "And there's a great view from this height."

They gazed out over the amazing panorama of the Kenyan plain. The flat landscape was broken up by clumps of bushes and the occasional acacia, its branches stretching like a fan towards the deep blue sky.

"There are animals wherever we look!" exclaimed Zoe, shading her eyes. "Zebra, deer, and that's a massive herd of wildebeest on the horizon."

"And giraffes feeding at those trees!" added Ben.

"Ahh! Look at those sweet little piglets!" cried Zoe, as a family of warthogs snuffled past, noses to the ground.

Ben raised his eyebrows. "Gooey overload, Zoe!" he complained.

They followed a well-trodden path through the yellow grass, towards some far distant dome-shaped huts surrounded by a thick fence.

"I told you this would be easy," called Ben. "I'm going to try and go faster." He squeezed the camel's flanks with his legs. Nothing happened. He squeezed a bit harder. With that the camel gave a deep-throated snort and bucked him off.

Ben hit the ground in a cloud of dust.

"It's not funny!" he grunted, rubbing his bottom as Zoe burst out laughing.

His camel blinked its long lashes and then began to plod towards the village. "After you," said Ben, as he followed on foot at a safe distance.

Finally, they reached the entrance to the village – not much more than a narrow gap in the thorny fence. Zoe persuaded her camel to kneel and then dismounted.

"That's a barrier to keep the elephants out," said Ben. "I read about it on the plane. Even though the Samburu care a lot about them they don't want them trampling their homes."

Zoe tied both camels securely to the fence, and tucked Wambua's package under her arm. They walked between the round huts with walls of upright branches and woven sticks that they could see were filled with dried mud. Stretched skins and grass mats formed the domed roofs. Women were squatting at pots over cooking fires and a group of men were tending their goats. They all wore cloths wrapped round them like skirts and strings of shiny beads hung round their heads, necks, wrists and from their ears. They looked up when they saw Ben and Zoe approaching, then lowered their heads to their tasks. No one greeted them, although some of the little children stared wide-eyed.

"These people don't look very friendly," Zoe whispered to Ben.

"Perhaps they're shy," he replied. "Let's put in our translators." He rummaged in his rucksack and peeled off the small earpiece from the side of his BUG. "Then if they talk amongst themselves, we'll understand what they're saying."

They slipped the earpieces in.

Ben and Zoe wandered around, trying in vain to approach any villager who passed, but they scuttled away, heads bowed.

"Nobody wants to talk to us," whispered Zoe. "And what's really strange is they're not even talking to each other."

She gave a sudden gasp. "Something bad happened here," she said, pointing beyond the goat pen. The blackened ruins of a hut stood stark against the blue sky.

"That looks like a recent fire," said Ben.

"Here's another burnt hut – and another,"

said Zoe, as they walked through the village. "How strange. It can't have been one fire – the huts in between are untouched."

A woman walked by, clutching a baby.

"Excuse me," said Zoe, holding up the parcel. "Wambua?"

The woman didn't look at her, but hastily pointed towards a goat pen nearby.

An old man was splashing water into a trough and the goats were nudging him eagerly. He spotted the package under Zoe's arm as the children approached him.

"From Runo," said Zoe with a smile.

"Thank you," said the old man. His face was painted with blue zigzags and his earlobes were pulled down by heavy bead earrings. "You are staying at the lodge?"

"We're on holiday," said Zoe, glad to find someone ready to talk. "We're with our tutor and she's sent us to find out all about elephants."

"They're such magnificent animals," added Ben. "Can you tell us more about them?"

The old man's face softened. "They are wonderful beasts," he said. "We are blessed with a herd that lives on the plain. It is led by a matriarch called Nyeupe – that means white in your language. She is much paler than the other elephants. She is nearly fifty years old now and a grandmother many times over."

He gestured for them to sit by a small fire. Nearby, a woman grinding corn in a wooden bowl gave them a nervous glance.

"Is it a big herd?" asked Zoe.

"Four grown females and two younger ... you would call them teenagers?" said Wambua. "And somewhere out there are two bull elephants. They do not live with the herd."

"Could you take us to see them?" said Ben.

For a moment Wambua's eyes lit up. "It is a wonderful trek. We walk for a day and make a camp by the Tulivu waterhole at nightfall, ready to see the elephants when they come to drink at first light. That is while the lake still has enough water, as it does now."

The woman suddenly called out to him in Samburu. Ben and Zoe heard her words translated through their earpieces.

"Be quiet, you foolish old man! Do you want to bring more trouble?"

Ben and Zoe forced themselves not to react. The woman had sounded very scared.

Wambua seemed to heed her warning, for he sighed heavily and shook his head.

"We don't take visitors there any more," he said sadly. He gave an involuntary glance over to the burnt huts.

Ben patted his pockets. "We'll pay well."

"It is not possible," said Wambua flatly.

Zoe decided to play the spoilt rich girl. "But I want to see a baby elephant," she whined.

"There is only one left," Wambua told her. "So it's not worth it. Now I must tend my goats. Goodbye."

He turned away.

Ben and Zoe got to their feet. "Thank you," called Ben and they began to walk back through the village.

39

A little girl came plodding across their path, waving her arm in front of her like an elephant's trunk.

"How sweet," said Zoe.

A little boy jumped up and followed the girl, pretending to be an elephant as well. He had a rope tied round his leg and was limping badly. He cried out in his own language.

"Wait for me, Mum!" The translated words came through loud and clear. "My leg hurts."

"Come on, baby," said the girl. "We're getting left behind."

Suddenly, two older boys rose up from behind a box, holding sticks to their shoulders like rifles.

"Bang… Bang!" they yelled and the two "elephants" fell to the ground.

Then they got up laughing.

"Now I'll put a snare on you," said the girl to one of the older boys. "And Pili and I are the hunters."

She started to untie the rope from her friend's leg. But at that moment one of the women came running over and the little girl froze, looking guilty.

"Stop that!" cried the woman. "I've told you before. No more talk of elephants! You don't know who's listening. Remember what happened last week."

She gave Ben and Zoe a scared glance and ushered the children inside a nearby hut.

"They were acting out a hunt!" said Ben. "A hunt where young elephants were being snared to slow them down. They must have overheard their parents talking."

"The baby and its mother are separated from the herd so they're easy to pick off," said Zoe. "How horrible. So hunters have snared poor Tomboi to get at his mum. The villagers seem too frightened to talk about it."

"I wonder if the burnt huts are connected with this," said Ben. "After all, something's stopping the villagers from having anything to do with the elephants."

"Then we've got to protect the herd for them," declared Zoe.

CHAPTER FOUR

The sun was low over the plain by the time Ben and Zoe got back to the lodge. Runo quickly sneaked their camels back to the compound.

"We have to set off to find Tomboi tomorrow," said Ben, as they made their way back to their room. "Wambua said the herd go to the waterhole every sunrise. If we set off early in the morning and camp out overnight we should get there at the right time."

"The sooner we sort out his leg the better,"

said Zoe. "We don't know when the hunt is going to be, but if we can get Tomboi fit, he won't be trailing the herd and the hunters will find it much harder to get him and his mum."

They were just crossing the lobby to collect their key from reception when Zoe grabbed her brother's arm.

"Recognize that man leaning on the desk?" she hissed.

Ben studied the tall, plump man in shorts and a T-shirt who was talking loudly in English to the hotel manager. "No."

"Look at his hat with all the badges and feathers on it," insisted Zoe. "We saw enough photos of him wearing it on that awful hunting site."

"Oh, yes!" said Ben. "It's that idiot who boasted he'd shot game on every continent."

"What was his name?" hissed Zoe. "It was all over the site."

Ben thought for a minute. "Hall! Frank
Hall."

They retrieved their key with its large
wooden rhino-shaped fob and let
themselves into their bedroom.

"It can't be a coincidence that a big-game
hunter turns up where elephants are being
shot illegally," said Ben, pacing up and down
between the two beds. "But we haven't got
any proof that's what he's here for."

45

"Which is where Uncle Stephen's OWL comes in," said Zoe eagerly. "We plant it on Mr Hall. Then we'll hear if he's up to anything." She dug the box that contained the OWL out of her backpack and opened it. "There's only one problem. When are we going to get the chance to attach it to him? And what do we attach it to?"

Ben frowned. "It needs to go wherever he goes."

"We can't exactly go up to him and slap it on his shirt!" said Zoe. "And besides, he won't be wearing the same things every day."

They thought for a moment.

"His hat!" cried Ben. "We could plant the OWL on that."

"Good plan!" said Zoe, slipping the little box into the pocket of her shorts. "But finding the right moment's going to be difficult."

"And I've got another plan," said Ben. "Dinner. I'm starving."

Ben and Zoe sat at a table on the wooden
deck of the restaurant, overlooking a small
lake. Citronella candles burned fiercely to
keep the mosquitoes at bay. The sun had
gone down behind the low hills to the west,
leaving a warm glow on the horizon.
Occasionally a security guard passed by, rifle
over his shoulder, watching in case any
predators came too close for comfort.

Every now and then there was a stir in the
restaurant as a nocturnal animal was spotted
coming for a drink at the lake.

"What's that?" said Zoe, as a small creature
with a bushy black-and-white striped tail
slunk up to the water's edge.

Ben got out his BUG and began to fiddle
with it under the table. "Genet cat," he read .
"Though interestingly it's not a cat, but a
member of the mongoose family."

"It's so cute," said Zoe. Ben rolled his eyes.

Eating their fish curry as slowly as they could, the children watched the diners come and go, but there was no sign of Frank Hall. Ben started playing with his BUG again.

"The BUG has identified caracal cries," he told Zoe, eyes shining. "You know, those lynx-like cats with the amazing pointed ears."

"Cool Gameboy you've got there," came a voice. Ben looked up. A boy of about twelve with short blond hair was grinning at them from the next table. "Have you got 'Alien Escape 4'?" As the boy got up to take a closer look, Ben quickly pressed a button and a decoy game flashed up on the screen.

"No, I've only got a football game so far." Ben showed him. "It's not that good." He slid the BUG quickly into his pocket.

"I don't think we'll be playing many computer games," said Zoe. "There's too much to see."

"It's great here, isn't it?" said the boy eagerly. "I've got a new camera and I can't wait to try it out. We're going on a trek later this week to photograph the wildlife. I'm hoping to get the big five. Lions, elephants, rhinos and buffaloes will be easy, but leopards are going to be harder."

"Making friends, Lester?" boomed a voice behind them.

Lester's manner changed abruptly. "Just chatting, Dad," he muttered.

Ben and Zoe looked round to see the newcomer.

It was Frank Hall.

CHAPTER FIVE

The big-game hunter flung his jacket on the back of his chair and sat down with a loud grunt, making Lester wince with embarrassment.

"I was just talking about our trek," the boy explained, sitting back down and fingering the flowers in the vase between them.

"You'll be part of a real man's world for a change," said his father. "Walking the plain like a bushman, roughing it in a tent, cooking your own food and—"

He stopped as Lester let out a wail of

horror and backed away from the flowers.

"What's the matter?" snapped Mr Hall.

"Spider," croaked Lester. "A great big one. On that petal!"

Red with anger, Mr Hall knocked the spider on to the table and squashed it with his fist. "Fuss about nothing," he grumbled, flicking the body away.

"Why did you kill it?" protested Lester.

Ben and Zoe buried their heads in their menus.

"Poor Lester," whispered Zoe, "having a dad like that."

"Whatever else Mr Hall's up to," said Ben, "at least he's taking his son on a photography expedition. Maybe that's the only reason he's here."

"We need to be sure," said Zoe, patting the pocket that contained the OWL. "Look, he hasn't got his hat with him."

"Then it must be in his room," said Ben.

"We can't go in there," whispered Zoe.

"We've got to," said Ben. "And for that we need the key. I can see the fob sticking out of his jacket pocket. I'll make a diversion and you grab it."

"Be careful," hissed Zoe.

"Trust me." Ben winked, getting to his feet. He sauntered past the Halls, who were studying their menus, and made for the dessert table. He placed two papayas and a mango on a plate and wove his way back. Just as he reached Lester and his father, he appeared to trip. The fruit rolled off the plate and bounced under their table.

"Oh dear!" gasped Ben. He dived beneath the cloth and crawled over their feet, chasing the lost fruit.

"What are you doing?" growled Frank Hall, pushing his chair back and peering under the table.

Ben rolled the mango towards Zoe across

the floor. She leaped from her seat and made a great show of scrabbling for it on the ground. At the same time she slipped her other hand deftly into Mr Hall's jacket pocket, removed the key and hid it up her sweatshirt sleeve.

Ben emerged from under the table, holding the papayas. "Got them!" he beamed.

"And here's the mango!" said Zoe, producing the fruit. "I'm sorry we disturbed you."

Lester started to laugh, but caught his father's eye and stopped.

"Dreadful behaviour!" growled Frank Hall. "You shouldn't be allowed in here on your own. Where are your parents?"

"Our parents aren't with us," said Zoe.

"Disgraceful! Kids on their own."

Lester looked down at the table in embarrassment.

"But our tutor's in her room," said Ben calmly. "She's not feeling well."

"Why didn't you have your meal with her?" grunted Mr Hall. "Then you wouldn't have bothered the rest of us."

"We're just going there now," Zoe put in

quickly. "The fruit's for her. Come on, Ben,"
she said, grabbing her brother by the arm.

Checking that the corridor was empty, Zoe
turned the key to room 212. The door
swung open on to a huge bedroom. All
around the walls were beautiful paintings of
lions, leopards and giraffes in their natural
surroundings. The children dived inside and
shut the door.

"Wow!" gasped Ben. "This is a lot posher
than our room."

On a desk in the corner sat a laptop and
some hunting magazines. Clothes were
slung on chairs and in the centre of the
four-poster bed was the hat.

"Let's get on with it and go," said Zoe
nervously. She threw down the key and the
mango on the bed and grabbed the hat.

She quickly positioned the OWL on the

front, between a green feather and a badge with "Hot shot!" emblazoned on it. Within seconds it was stuck fast. She'd just put the hat back on the bed when they heard voices outside the door.

"I'm certain I had the key with me." It was Mr Hall!

"It is not a problem, sir." The children recognized the voice of the receptionist and heard a key sliding into the lock. "I have the master key."

"Quick," hissed Ben. "Hide!"

The children dived under the bed.

"The mango!" gasped Zoe. "I've left it with the key!" She scrambled out and retrieved the telltale fruit.

She slid back just as the door opened.

They heard an exclamation of surprise and saw Mr Hall's sandalled feet striding over towards them.

The children looked at each other, eyes

wide in the dark. Had he seen Zoe?

But then Frank Hall let out a gruff laugh. "Here it is!" He stopped at the bedside, his feet only centimetres from their faces. There was a rattle as he picked up the key, then the chink of coins. He moved away from the bed. "Take that for your trouble."

"Thank you, sir." The door closed softly as the receptionist left with his tip.

"Can we stay here and watch telly?" they heard Lester plead. "I'm tired."

"We haven't come all this way for you to watch television," declared his father. "We're going to talk to Chitundu now. And he asked to have a good look at the hunting badges on my hat," he added, picking up his hat and putting it on.

"Who's Chitundu?"

"Don't you ever listen?" said Mr Hall, exasperated. "I told you about him. He's a Samburu from the local village – although he lives at the hotel now. He's the one taking us on this expedition. I want him to meet you."

"I remember," muttered Lester. "But he'll be too busy to see us, won't he? You said he works as a chef here and dinner's still being served."

"He'll be there," said Mr Hall. "But we

don't let on to anyone that he's involved with our trip. Not fair on him if the lodge found he was working a sideline. Their employees aren't meant to make extra money out of the guests."

"So how can Chitundu come with us without the lodge knowing?" persisted Lester.

"Use your head, lad," scoffed his father. "He's taking a few days off – unpaid, of course – so they won't know anything about it." He gave his gruff laugh. "He'll get more than enough money from me to make up for it."

He moved towards the door. "Let's go," he said. "Bring your camera to show him."

Lester sighed. They heard his hurried footsteps as he went into his room then back to join his father. Finally the door clicked shut.

Ben and Zoe waited for a moment, listening hard. Then they slid out from their hiding place.

"I thought I was going to squash the papayas." Ben grinned. "Shame to ruin our afters—" He broke off. A key was turning in the lock again. They only just had time to disappear back under the bed before Lester ran in.

"I'm going on down, Lester," came Frank Hall's grumbling tones from the corridor. "Don't be long."

"I won't be," his son called back sulkily. "I just need my camera battery."

Ben and Zoe heard Lester zip open a bag. It sounded as if he was having trouble with the camera. Then the battery dropped with a clatter on to the wooden floor.

It bounced and slid right under the bed, coming to rest between Ben and Zoe.

They shrank as far away as they could as Lester got down on his knees. They hardly dared breathe. Any moment now they were going to be discovered.

CHAPTER SIX

Ben quickly rolled on to his back, pulled out his BUG and swiftly tapped at the keys. As Lester's hand felt further under the bed the sound of a hissing snake burst out from Ben's BUG. Lester gave a terrified cry and his hand quickly withdrew. They saw his feet rushing in a mad panic to the door. It slammed shut behind him.

"How did you know Lester was scared of snakes?" breathed Zoe.

Ben shrugged as he pulled himself out from his hiding place. "A lucky guess!

I remembered how frightened he was by the spider."

"We'd better go before Mr Hall sends someone to get rid of the snake," said Zoe.

Back in their own room, Ben threw the papayas on to the dressing table. "This trek seems really hush-hush. What if we're right about the hunt?" he said breathlessly. "Why all the secrecy if they're just going on a photography expedition?"

"Slow down with your theories!" said Zoe. "Neither of them mentioned a hunt. All we know is Chitundu's not meant to be doing extra work while he's employed at the lodge. And Lester took his camera to show him. It might really be a photography expedition."

"Let's listen in on the OWL," said Ben. He tapped the OWL key on his BUG. The screen flickered and an image of glowing lights, palm trees and tables appeared.

"They're in the corner of the courtyard," said Zoe, looking over her brother's shoulder. "There doesn't seem to be anyone sitting near them. But I can't see if they're with this Chitundu. Can you hear anything?"

"I could if you kept quiet!" joked Ben.

Zoe poked out her tongue at him.

The children sat on Zoe's bed in silence, listening. At first all they could make out was the low murmur of voices. Then the screen was blocked by a green Amani Lodge uniform.

"Chitundu!" they heard Mr Hall say. "Sit down."

"I only have a moment." The voice was quiet, with an accent similar to Runo's and his grandfather's. "My boss is around somewhere."

"He won't have anything to complain about. After all, you're simply telling us the recipe for that delicious *Nyama Choma* we

had tonight, aren't you?" Mr Hall sounded
in a jolly mood. He dropped his voice.
"This is my son, Lester. He'll be coming
with us. Is everything ready?"

"It is. I have the … equipment and I can
take some holiday in three days' time."

The speaker leaned forwards, his hands
pressed on to the table, and now Ben and
Zoe could see his face on their BUG screen.
He was young, with very short black hair.
"I am pleased to meet you, Lester." He
pointed to something on the table and his
smile widened. "I see you have your camera
– very nice, but I will bring something else
to help you with your 'shots'."

The image swung round to show Lester examining his camera.

"Cheer up, boy!" said his father. "Get yourself a lemonade while Chitundu and I discuss the boring details." Lester scraped back his seat and stomped off. As soon as he'd gone, Mr Hall turned back to Chitundu.

"I hope you have something good for me, too," he said earnestly, "as I wasn't able to bring my own."

Chitundu looked around him, checking there was no one in earshot. "Highest velocity I could get, with a nice heavy cartridge," he answered smoothly. "It will go through bone as if it's butter. I have hidden your 'equipment' near the waterhole so you won't be seen carrying it. Of course I will have to carry something to protect us. But this shouldn't arouse any suspicion."

Ben and Zoe tensed and listened intently

from the safety of their room.

"And the calf will be very slow by then," Chitundu went on, with a smug smile. "It is days since I snared him. He and his mother will be well behind the herd and ripe for picking."

"So *he's* the one behind the elephant killings," said Ben through gritted teeth.

"Just like the children in the village were acting out," added Zoe.

"I bag the mother." Mr Hall sounded very pleased with himself. "And Lester gets the youngster. His first kill. But remember it's to stay a surprise for him until we're well on our way."

"I will not forget," said Chitundu gravely. "And remember our agreement. You get the heads. I get the bush meat."

"Of course," said Mr Hall.

"This is awful!" gasped Zoe, thumping her pillow in anger.

Chitundu was getting up to go. "I have to get back to the kitchen."

"Thank you for the recipe," said Mr Hall loudly. "I know it's going to be a success."

The image suddenly swung round to Lester, approaching with his lemonade.

"I thought you said my camera was really good, Dad," he complained. "Why does Chitundu want to give me a different one?"

"That was just a joke," said his father quickly. "Remember Chitundu's an expert at this sort of thing. I expect he's got a special zoom lens you can borrow. Stop grumbling!"

Ben shut down the image.

"Now we know who our hunters are!" he said. "And we've got three days before they set off."

He checked the satellite map on his BUG. "The waterhole Wambua told us about is south-east of here," he told his sister.

"He said it was a day's walk, so if we leave before first light tomorrow, like we planned, we'll be at the waterhole well in time."

Zoe began to stow the sleeping bags and food rations in their backpacks ready for the trek.

"Do you think Tomboi will have the chance to recover and rejoin the herd?" she suddenly burst out. "And won't the hunters be able to track him down anyway?"

"I'll report to Uncle Stephen," said Ben. "Now we know the hunting party will be setting out in three days' time he can alert the authorities. That will give them plenty of time to organize how to catch them in the act."

He pressed the hot key on his BUG that put him straight through to Wild HQ.

"What news?" came their godfather's eager voice.

Ben quickly told him about planting the
OWL, and reported everything they'd
heard. "So you'll get the Kenya Wildlife
Service to arrest the hunters?" he finished.

"It's not as easy as that, Ben," Dr Fisher
replied. "This Chitundu's been clever.
There's no evidence linking him to the
hunt – and we can't tell anyone that you
heard the conversation over a secret piece
of Wild equipment. Once you've sorted out

Tomboi, keep tracking Hall's movements and let me know when the hunters are getting near the waterhole. I'll make sure the Kenya Wildlife Service get wind of it. Over and out."

Zoe put the medical kit, torches, water bottles, night-vision goggles and binoculars into the backpacks.

"Tranquillizer guns on the top, just in case," she said, zipping up the bags. "Here we come, Tomboi."

CHAPTER SEVEN

Zoe woke to the sound of her alarm buzzing in her ear. She staggered out of bed in the dark and shook Ben. He was always hard to wake – especially at five thirty in the morning. By the time he'd pulled on his clothes his sister was ready by the door, checking the satellite map on her BUG.

They crept down the dim corridor, trying not to make the wooden floor creak.

At last the big double doors at the front of the softly lit lobby came into view.

"I can't see anyone on Reception,"

said Zoe. "Let's go – oof!"

Someone came round the corner and ran straight into her. It was Lester Hall. He had his camera slung round his neck and looked as if he'd pulled on his clothes in a hurry.

"Sorry," he mumbled, scratching his tousled head. "I'm not really awake."

"And we thought we were the only ones up!" said Ben, trying to sound relaxed and friendly. "Going somewhere nice?"

Lester yawned. "My dad's taking me on a photo expedition. But I didn't think he'd be dragging me out of bed in the middle of the night!"

Ben and Zoe stared at him, trying to keep the look of shock from their faces. The hunt was setting out today!

"What are you two doing up so early?" came a familiar voice, and Mr Hall strode into view.

He was kitted out for his expedition, from
his state-of-the-art trekking boots to his
expensive binoculars and his decorated hat.
Hands on hips, he looked Ben and Zoe up
and down, taking in their backpacks. He
poked a finger at them. "I get it. Sneaking
out while your tutor's ill. I bet she'd like to
know what you're up to."

"No," protested Zoe. "We—"

"I'm obliged to let the hotel know that you two are heading off on your own!" Mr Hall interrupted. "They won't want to send out a search party because a pair of stupid kids have been eaten by lions."

"Our tutor's coming with us," Ben assured him. "She's better now. We're just waiting for her."

"She knows this area well," Zoe took up the hastily improvised story. "She lived here when she was a girl." She could feel her heart thumping. Would Mr Hall believe them?

Mr Hall humphed. "That's all right then." A brief look of concern flickered over his face. "Where exactly are you going?"

Ben thought quickly. "To the village," he said. "Our tutor wants us to see a whole day in the life of the village."

Frank Hall forced a thin smile. The children saw he was relieved they wouldn't be going in his direction. "Come on, Lester," he grunted. "We've wasted enough time. Let's get going. I've ordered us some breakfast. We've got a long trek ahead so we'll need the energy."

The yawning boy traipsed off after his dad.

"This is a disaster!" whispered Zoe. "We thought we'd have three days before the hunters started out. Why have they changed their plans all of a sudden?"

"We can't worry about that now," replied Ben. "Our mission is to save Tomboi, and that means getting there before the hunters and sorting out his leg."

"And letting Uncle Stephen know that the hunt is on so he can alert the Kenya Wildlife Service," added Zoe. "Come on, we can tell him on our way."

Sneaking through the spotlit lodge grounds, the children dived behind a hippopotamus statue as an armed security guard walked past. Dawn was just breaking and the air was still cold.

"We've got to find a new route," said Ben. "And that's going to be hard. You can see a long way on the plain because it's so flat. We'll easily be spotted if we're anywhere near the hunting party." He called up a satellite picture of the area. A tiny red light pulsed from the lodge. "They're in the dining room."

"Let's hope it's a huge breakfast that will take them ages to eat," said Zoe.

"And that Frank Hall will be so stuffed he'll hardly be able to walk." Ben laughed and zoomed the map out until the waterhole appeared. "I know we should be heading south-east," he muttered, "but if we go south-west to start with, there's more cover."

"You're right." Zoe nodded as she looked over his shoulder. "There are clumps of trees there…" She pointed. "…And there."

"Then we cut south-east through that outcrop of rocks and finally get to the undergrowth near the waterhole," said Ben. "That's a good hiding place to wait for the elephants tomorrow morning. We'll camp somewhere on the way."

"But we'll have to set a good pace," said Zoe. "This detour makes our trek longer than theirs."

Ben tapped away at some keys on his BUG. "I've sent a message to Uncle Stephen to let him know the change of plan."

"Tranquillizer guns at the ready," added Zoe, nodding towards a large sign – DO NOT PROCEED UNACCOMPANIED BEYOND THIS POINT. "And scent dispersers on so we don't smell tempting to predators."

When the coast was clear they slipped out of the lodge grounds. Ben checked the map on his BUG and gestured for Zoe to follow.

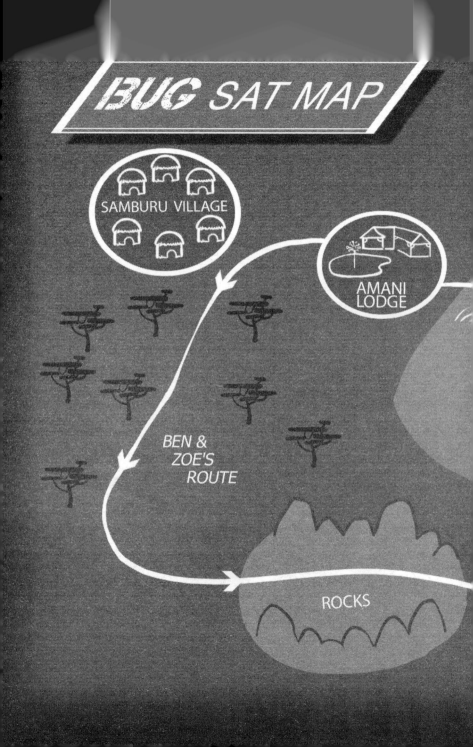

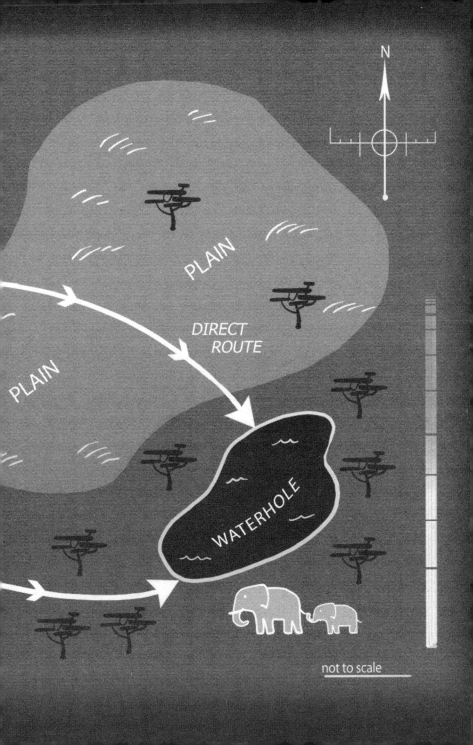

Skirting round the lodge, Ben and Zoe drank in the spectacular view of the plain bathed in the early morning sun. The flat land stretched away towards the snow-capped Mount Kenya in the far distance. Trees grew here and there – tall fanned acacias and thick-trunked baobabs.

The children moved quickly, darting for the cover of trees where they could. As the sun began to warm the arid land, the plain woke up. Herds of zebra and wildebeest grazed on the open grass and giraffes lolloped along as if chasing each other.

"Look over there," gasped Ben. "By those trees. Awesome! Our first sign of an elephant!"

"It's huge!" said Zoe, wide-eyed. "It couldn't be part of our herd, could it?"

"It's a male," said Ben. "Remember Wambua told us they live alone."

The bull elephant stamped about among

the trees, his head tossing and trunk swinging irritably.

"He looks bad-tempered," said Zoe. "Good thing we're nowhere near him."

Ben came to a sudden halt. "What's that over there?" he said, pointing at the far distance. "To the east. Something's moving and I don't think it's an animal." He threw himself flat on the ground, pulling Zoe with him.

Zoe grabbed her binoculars and focused them. "It's the hunting party. We were in full view."

"That was close!" panted Ben. "Did they see us?"

"I'll find out," said Zoe, calling up her OWL.

"I did see something," they heard Mr Hall insist. "It looked like people."

"I cannot see anything," came Chitundu's voice. "I expect it was an animal."

"Hope so," grunted the hunter, "for your sake."

"Now we've stopped can I take some photos?" asked Lester. "We've been going so fast I haven't managed to take one yet."

"You'll get some good shots later." His father chuckled.

"We must be more careful," said Zoe. She studied the map on her BUG. "We should go further west."

They took the new route, seeking high grass and thick bushes whenever possible.

Suddenly, there was a tremendous crashing in the bushes ahead of them and the bull elephant burst out into the open. He stamped his front feet, blowing angrily through his trunk. The children stopped, not daring to take another step.

"Stay still," whispered Ben. "He might ignore us."

They could hear a low growling noise as

the elephant shook his head. Then he raised his trunk and gave a tremendous trumpet of rage.

"Run!" cried Zoe, as the elephant began to charge.

CHAPTER EIGHT

The elephant pounded towards them, his huge ears outstretched.

Ben caught his sister's arm as she turned to flee.

"Just step into the thick bushes," he said quietly. "Move slowly and don't make eye contact."

Although every fibre of her body was telling her to run, Zoe obeyed. She knew she could trust Ben. She had to steel herself not to check over her shoulder at the six thousand kilos of charging mammal.

The sound of thundering feet grew closer. Leaves and branches flew into the air as the bull elephant pushed through the bushes towards the children's hiding place.

Then, as suddenly as it had started, the thudding stopped and they could hear loud snorts. The elephant was standing a short distance away, tossing his head. At last he tramped off, his trunk swinging from side to side.

"It was just a dummy charge," said Ben. "Thought as much. He had his ears forward. Anyone who knows anything about elephants could have told you."

Zoe gawped at him. Ben managed to keep a straight face for about five seconds, then he burst out laughing.

"I read about it on the plane," he confessed. "Ears forward and a lot of noise means the elephant is just showing us who's boss. It's when his ears are back and he's

silent that you've got to worry." His face
took on a look of mock seriousness and he
scratched his chin thoughtfully. "Or is it the
other way round?" He dodged as Zoe gave
him a friendly punch.

At last they reached an outcrop of rocks
that pushed up through the yellow grass.

"Food time," said Ben, flopping down
under the welcome shade of an overhanging
ledge. He unwrapped an energy bar.

"They've stopped as well," said Zoe,
watching the screen on her BUG.

Mr Hall was tucking into a plateful of food, which they saw each time he dipped his head to shovel up another forkful.

"Eat up, boy!" he said through a mouth full of food. "This is top rate tucker!"

For a moment Lester came into shot. He was toying miserably with the food on his plate.

"Tell him what we've got in store for tomorrow, Chitundu," barked Mr Hall. "That'll bring a smile to his face."

Chitundu appeared now, squatting a little way from his guests and looking pleased with himself.

"We will make camp tonight and at first light tomorrow we will reach the elephants where they go to drink," he said. "I have lamed a calf by throwing a bolas at him. The snare is cutting into his leg and slowing him down."

"Disgusting man!" hissed Zoe, as

Chitundu continued to outline his plan.

"His mother will not leave him so they are gradually getting further behind the herd. It will be easy for your father to shoot her. She is a magnificent beast – good tusks."

"Excellent!" came Mr Hall's voice. He sounded excited. "She'll get pride of place in my hallway."

"What do you mean?" came an appalled shout. Lester was staring at his father, a look of shock on his face. "You didn't say you were going to shoot anything," he went on. "We're here to photograph the animals close up, aren't we?"

"Yes." The scene moved up and down as Mr Hall nodded his head. "Nice and close!"

Zoe felt sick at his smug tone.

Lester went on. "I don't want to hunt! I've told you loads of times, but you never listen. It's illegal here in Kenya anyway."

"That makes it more of a thrill," came Mr Hall's voice. "Anyway, Chitundu's taken care of all that, haven't you."

"Yes, sir." Chitundu was grinning at his boss.

"No one suspects a thing, do they?" said Mr Hall. "Although I did wonder why you brought the trek forwards suddenly. There's no problem, is there?"

"No," said Chitundu. "The only reason we set out this morning is because I had to change my leave with one of the other chefs."

"What about the Samburu?" asked Mr Hall. "Do they know what's going on?"

"They will not bother us." Chitundu was smirking. "I have been doing this for a while now. The people in my village claim to have some stupid bond with the elephants and there were protests at first, but I got some ... friends to pay them a visit. A few huts got burned, and they learned the errors of their ways."

Zoe turned to Ben. "So that's what happened at the Samburu village," she said.

Ben nodded. "It certainly explains why the tribespeople were so frightened."

They turned back to the screen as Lester spoke.

"This is awful, Dad." He'd come up close to his father. "I don't want anything to do with it."

"Don't be a wimp! We've got a special treat for you. Haven't we, Chitundu?"

"I have a gun especially for your height and weight," he answered. "The young calf will be barely able to move now with that bad leg. He will be perfect for your first kill."

"You're not getting Tomboi," Ben muttered. "Not if we get there first."

"I don't like it." Lester sounded scared.

"You need to toughen up, son," Mr Hall said brusquely. "And I know just how to do it. I'll give you a boxing lesson. It'll make you strong and sharpen up your reflexes. Then you'll be as good a hunter as me."

"I don't want to."

Ben and Zoe could see Lester backing away from his father.

"Nonsense! Take a swing!"

"No! Leave me alone—"

"Put your fists up, boy!" came Mr Hall's challenge. He seemed to lunge at his son and the next minute the scene on the BUG shook and spun.

Zoe gasped. "His hat's fallen off..." She and Ben got a sudden view of a huge boot sole, then there was a nasty crunching sound and the screen went black. They looked at each other in utter dismay.

"He's trodden on it!" cried Ben. "He's broken the OWL!"

"This is serious!" said Zoe. "We can't keep track of them now. We won't know how far they've got."

"Then we're going to have to pick up our pace," said Ben. "I'll message Uncle Stephen to let him know we've lost our link."

By nightfall Ben and Zoe were exhausted. They'd ignored their aching legs and pushed on until the sky was glowing red and the sun was a huge orange ball on the horizon. The heat of the day was already beginning to cool.

"We should stop," said Ben. "We need to sleep."

"But there's no shelter here," protested Zoe. "Look, over there. That small rise in the ground. It's not far. We can lie in our sleeping bags and still see across the plain."

"We won't be able to light a fire up there, though," said Ben, as they carried on. "It'll be spotted. Lucky our sleeping bags are warm."

When they reached the little hillock, Ben shook out the ultra thin sleeping bags – clever inventions of their godfather's. They made themselves as comfortable as they could on the hard ground.

Zoe handed him an energy bar. "Fish and chips!" She grinned. "Followed by chocolate ice cream!"

"I wish!" groaned Ben.

Supper over, they lay down, listening to the rustling of animals in the grass, the howls of wild dogs and the manic laughing call of hyenas.

Ben checked his BUG. "Just making sure the scent disperser's still on," he said. "Most of the predators around here like to hunt at night."

Zoe stared up at the thousands of stars, sharp and bright against the deep black sky. Eventually, she fell into a troubled sleep, full of guns and dying elephants.

"Zoe!"

She woke with a start.

"Don't move!"

Ben was lying stock still beside her. It was very dark and her breath came out in clouds in the cold air. And then she saw it. An even darker shape padding around their backpacks, almost close enough to touch. They had a visitor – a huge, hungry-looking lioness.

CHAPTER NINE

Ben and Zoe listened to the soft snuffling of the lioness as she prowled around them. The lioness padded up and down, pushing at their backpacks with her nose. One toppled as she touched it and she sprang back, snarling. Zoe's eyes flickered with terror, but she didn't dare move, not even to reach for her tranquillizer gun.

Now the lioness was out of their view, but they could hear a strange scratching sound, then a "bleep". Zoe's heart sank as she realized that the lioness must be pawing at

her BUG! If she damaged it the scent
disperser might stop working – then she'd
be sure to catch their scent. Zoe could feel
panic rising in her chest. *Remember your
Wild training*, she told herself. *Don't move.
Slow, shallow breathing.*

Ben lay still. He sensed that Zoe was getting desperate, but there was nothing he could do. Now the lioness's huge head came into his view, looming over him. He closed his eyes as her muzzle grew closer and closer. He could feel her hot breath on his face. It smelt of blood. Her nose touched his cheek. It was strange how gentle this ferocious animal was being when at any minute it could… Ben shut out the thought.

Then they heard a distant bleating sound. The lioness whipped round and sped off towards it. Alarmed cries and the pounding of hooves filled the air.

For a moment neither Ben nor Zoe moved. At last they sat up and stared anxiously into the dark, looking for any signs of the lioness returning.

Ben reached out for Zoe's BUG. "Yuck! It's got lion slobber on it, but at least it's still working."

"I was so frightened," breathed Zoe shakily. "I nearly gave us away."

Her brother put his arm round her. "You've just avoided being eaten by the top predator in Africa," he said. "I reckon it's OK to be scared."

Zoe gave him a grateful smile. "I hope whatever it was that was making that noise got away."

"Just think of the lioness as an alarm clock," Ben went on. "I've never woken up so quickly in my life!"

"Let's get going," said Zoe, rubbing her arms to warm herself. "The hunters won't be up yet, so we'll gain some time. Due east now, to the waterhole." She pulled out their small, lightweight night-vision goggles and handed a pair to Ben.

Ben nodded and tossed her a cereal bar.

"You can't be hungry already!" exclaimed Zoe. "It's only four o'clock!"

"Got to have breakfast," declared Ben.

The night world turned green as they put on their goggles. They trod as softly as possible between the clearly defined trees and deep grasses, checking the satellite map as they went.

"What's that sound?" asked Ben suddenly, clutching at Zoe's backpack strap. "I can hear a sort of hissing ahead. And look, it's like the ground's moving!"

The children backed away. A wide column of ants was marching along, completely blocking their path. It stretched endlessly in both directions. The ants scrambled over sticks and leaves in their way, not stopping for an instant. Every now and then one or two larger, square-headed ants could be seen.

"They must be the soldier ants of the colony," whispered Zoe, pointing down at them. "They're as long as my finger."

Ben tapped a key on his BUG and held it towards the seething mass of insects. The hissing sound was even louder now.

"At least it wasn't a snake," said Zoe in relief. "It must just be the noise of them marching. Can we get through the column?"

Her brother shook his head. "Dorylus," he read. "Also known as safari ants."

At that moment a large stray centipede scuttled towards the column. The nearest ants immediately swarmed all over it. Soon it stopped writhing and its body was eaten within seconds. Zoe shuddered. "We'd better wait until they've all gone."

Ben laughed. "There's probably millions of them. We'll be here for days!"

"If only those acacia trees were growing nearer each other," said Zoe. "We could use them as a bridge."

"And if there were vines we could do a Tarzan swing right over the ants," joked Ben. "No point wasting any more time. Maybe we can get across further along."

They trudged alongside the ants, keeping a safe distance. They saw other insects that were unwise enough to get close being engulfed and eaten in a flash.

"It's like they have their route and they're going to stick to it," said Ben.

They could see the wide column of ants weaving its way across the rough open ground into the dark distance.

"This isn't working," said Zoe anxiously, checking the map on the BUG. "They're heading south now and we need to go east. They're pushing us off our route. We have to cross them somehow or it'll be too late by the time we get to the waterhole."

"We can't yet," said Ben. "All we can do is carry on."

"Look!" Zoe was staring ahead. "The trees here are growing closer together. Follow me." She grasped the trunk of the nearest one and pulled herself up into its branches. Ben could see that its leaves interlaced with a smaller tree on the other side of the ant column.

Soon Zoe was hanging by her arms from a

high branch, which shook dangerously as
she moved. Then she leaned out and
grasped a branch from the smaller tree.
It seemed sturdy enough. "Here goes!"

The branch sunk under her weight as she
swung on to it and for a moment she
thought she was going to lose her grip. She
glanced down at the teeming river of ants,
remembering what happened to the
centipede that had got in their way. It
didn't bear thinking about. Knuckles white,
she held on tightly and made it to the
trunk, hand over hand. She jumped to the
ground, a look of triumph on her face.

"Nothing to it!" she called.

Ben shinned up the trunk and edged
across until he was hanging from the smaller
tree. The branch began to creak ominously.

"Hurry!" called Zoe. "It's going to break."

"Nearly there," Ben assured her as he
scrabbled along.

A loud crack suddenly split the air and the branch tore away from the trunk. Ben plummeted downwards, kicking madly to land clear of the column of deadly insects. He rolled over as he landed and stood up quickly.

"That was close!" he gasped. Then he leaped in pain and clutched his arm. "Ow!"

Zoe could see a large ant on Ben's elbow. Then she spotted two more, higher up his arm. She dashed them off his skin, leaving dark marks. Ben yelped each time.

"It's OK," she said. "They've gone."

"Thanks," groaned Ben, examining the bites. "Pity they left their teeth behind!"

Zoe shone her torch. Stuck deep in Ben's skin were three sets of tiny ant fangs. She tried to pull them out, but Ben yanked his arm away with a cry. "Too painful," he told her. "Anyway, there's no time for this now."

Zoe ignored him and took out the first-aid kit from her backpack. She scanned the labels in the torchlight. "Analgesic cream," she said, unscrewing the lid. "It's very strong and it'll take away the pain." Without waiting for a reply, she rubbed it on to his arm and then they set off.

Finally the children emerged from the trees,
just as the first rays of dawn light were
spreading over the open ground. They took
off their night-vision goggles and stowed
them away. Within a few minutes the great
yellow ball of the sun was clear of the
horizon. Birds started their dawn chorus and
a group of baboons skittered away towards
the trees as the children approached. A herd
of buffalo meandered by, and a group of
impalas chewed peacefully and watched.

Beyond was the white-capped peak of the
distant mountain. And in front of them was
the waterhole, rippling gently in the sunlight.

"We've made it!" gasped Ben. "And we've
beaten the hunters."

"And look – the herd is coming!" said
Zoe in excitement.

The children crouched in the dense
undergrowth, watching the line of elephants
lumbering towards the pool's edge.

"That must be Nyeupe, the matriarch, up
in front," Ben whispered, pointing to a huge
pale-looking elephant with extra baggy skin.

"I can't see a calf so Tomboi and his mother must be quite a way behind," said Zoe.

The matriarch gave a snort and waded into the pool. Others followed, sucking up the water and squirting it into their mouths.

Zoe sighed with delight as two of the elephants on the bank entwined their trunks playfully round each other.

"No time to go gooey!" declared Ben. "We still have to intercept Tomboi and his mum. They must be coming from the same direction as the rest. If we go round the northern edge of the water, behind the thickest trees over there, we should be able to meet them as they try to catch up with the herd."

The children got up as slowly as they could and made for the bushes where the elephants had come from.

"This has to be their regular route," said Ben, staring at the path through the trees.

"Look how the ground's trodden down."

"Tomboi must be in real trouble with that snare," whispered Zoe. "He's not even in sight yet. What if it's already badly infected?"

Just then, Ben's BUG vibrated. "It's Uncle Stephen," he said.

"I'm afraid there's been a bit of a problem," came their godfather's voice. He sounded worried. "The Kenya Wildlife Service may not get to the waterhole in time."

"It's up to us then," said Ben.

"Don't try any heroics. This could be really nasty – just try and get some footage of the hunters on your BUGs that we can pass off as a tourist video. Over and out."

Zoe turned to Ben. "We've still got to try and stop them!"

Suddenly, a deafening shot rang out.

"The hunters!" gasped Zoe. "They're here!"

CHAPTER TEN

Ben and Zoe raced along the elephant track towards the sound.

Rounding a baobab tree they drew back at the terrible scene in front of their eyes.

A full-grown elephant cow lay on her side. Blood was seeping from a wound in her flank, forming a dark red pool under her belly. She wasn't moving. Her young calf stood over her, bellowing mournfully and desperately trying to raise her with his little trunk. The children could see he had a wire wrapped around his back

leg and the wound was oozing yellow pus.
The calf looked almost too weak to
stand.

"It's Tomboi!" gulped Zoe. "And they've
shot his mother. We have to stop them
getting him as well."

She leaped forwards and Ben quickly
pulled her back behind the tree. "Stay
here!" he whispered. "The hunters will
see us."

But the little calf's pitiful cries were too
much for Zoe. "We can't just sit and
watch!" She tried to control the sobs rising
in her throat.

"We have to wait," insisted Ben. "It's too
dangerous."

The sound of angry yelling reached them
from somewhere nearby.

"You idiot, Lester, grabbing my arm
like that! You put me off my aim." They
recognized Frank Hall's voice.

"Don't worry, Mr Hall," Chitundu put in quickly. "It was a really professional shot. I'm sure you killed her. Let me check."

"You shouldn't have done it, Dad!" They heard Lester yell back. "It's barbaric!"

"Rubbish, boy. This is sport," snapped his father. "Now it's your turn. Here's your gun. Hold it like Chitundu showed you. The calf's a sitting target. Don't you let me down!"

"I told you, I won't do it!" The boy was almost sobbing now. "You can't make me."

"Good for Lester!" muttered Ben through gritted teeth.

"Look, Ben," breathed Zoe, edging round the tree trunk. "The mother's chest is moving!" She squeezed her brother's arm and smiled. "She's alive! Maybe we weren't too late! As soon as the hunters leave we'll go and—"

The children froze as Chitundu walked
towards Tomboi's mother, ignoring the
argument going on in the clearing behind
him, his rifle slung over his shoulder.

Ben put his hand on Zoe's. "I bet Chitundu's going to finish the job. Hall wants his trophy."

Zoe's eyes widened in fear. "Then we have to do something!" she said desperately.

"We wait for our chance, Zoe. I know it's hard, but if he sees us Chitundu might shoot us. He won't want witnesses. We may be able to do something for Tomboi at least." Ben beckoned to his sister and they peered round the tree. Now they could see the father and son. To their amazement Frank Hall was trying to wrestle the gun from Lester, a look of fury on his face. His battered hat had fallen to the ground.

Zoe whipped out her BUG and held it up, videoing the whole scene. She swung it round until Chitundu came into view next to the fallen elephant.

"Now we've got evidence," she said grimly.

"The thing's practically dead already with that bad leg," growled Mr Hall. "If you're not man enough to shoot it – I will."

"Don't you dare," shouted Lester. "I won't let you!" He was struggling with his father as if his life depended on it.

Ben turned to watch Chitundu. The hunter was crouching next to the mother elephant. Bellowing in panic, Tomboi began to headbutt him and Chitundu repeatedly pushed him away. He reached for his gun.

"I was right," muttered Ben, watching the man take a thin tube from a pouch on his belt. "He's got a silencer. He's going to finish her off."

Zoe put down her BUG and fumbled in her backpack. "I'm going to shoot him with the tranquillizer," she hissed.

But as she aimed the gun at Chitundu, Ben pulled her arm down.

"What are you doing?" she demanded. "I'm only going to knock him out."

"The dose is for a young elephant – not a man." Ben took the gun from her hand. "You might kill him!"

"You're right," Zoe said helplessly. "What can we do?"

"We could get the other elephants to come," gasped Ben. "If they knew these two were in trouble, they'd be on their way."

"But they're probably too far off to hear," sighed Zoe.

"Not if I amplify Tomboi's call," said Ben. He held up his BUG and pressed record as Tomboi gave another desperate bellow.

The little calf settled at his mother's side. With a huge effort the elephant cow raised her trunk and lovingly touched her baby's face. Then she lay still.

"Is it too late?" gulped Zoe.

"Not for Tomboi," said Ben. He turned up the BUG volume and played it back. The sound blasted into the air. Chitundu whipped round, trying to work out where it was coming from.

"That's too close to be an elephant," he muttered. He began to step purposefully towards their hiding place.

Ben and Zoe slithered backwards, desperate to keep hidden. Using the barrel of his gun, Chitundu smashed leaves and branches aside. He was coming closer. If they broke cover they knew he'd see them, and if they stayed where they were, he'd find them for sure. They were trapped.

Only a thin curtain of leaves separated them from the hunter now.

"Is there someone there?" growled Chitundu, raising his gun to his shoulder.

Ben and Zoe froze.

At that moment a deafening gunshot rang out followed by an angry curse. Chitundu fought his way back through the undergrowth. The children followed, just in time to see Lester, white with shock, holding his gun limply in one hand. Mr Hall was writhing on the ground, clutching his boot.

"You've shot me, you imbecile!" he groaned. "Don't just stand there. Get me to a hospital. I'm losing blood."

"Now he knows how the elephants feel!" said Ben vehemently. "Lester's done us a favour. They'll have to go back to the

lodge now. The minute they're out of the
way we'll be able to get to Tomboi."

Chitundu took the gun from Lester and
laid it on the ground. He knelt next to his
client.

"Where is the wound?" he asked urgently.

"My foot!" Mr Hall croaked. "My own
son shot me, the idiot."

"I didn't mean to, Dad," said Lester
shakily.

Frank Hall gave a yelp as Chitundu removed his boot and sock. "It is not serious," Chitundu told him. "The bullet just grazed your big toe. It's hardly bleeding. I will dress it."

The colour rushed back to Lester's face and he grinned with relief.

But his father rounded on him. "I don't know why you're so pleased with yourself," he snapped, wincing as Chitundu started to clean his wound. "You've ruined the whole hunt. Give me the gun. I'll see to the calf."

Ben and Zoe stared at each other. The nightmare wasn't over after all.

But suddenly Chitundu looked up. He was listening intently to distant sounds from along the track. "We can't risk staying any longer," he said. "The rest of the herd is coming."

"Fantastic!" whispered Zoe. "Your plan worked, Ben."

"Even though we nearly got shot," added Ben.

Mr Hall staggered to his feet. "I can't walk all the way back," he insisted crossly. "You'll have to call a jeep."

"There's no time," Chitundu replied. "It's too dangerous to wait here." He took Mr Hall firmly by the arm and helped him limp off.

The minute they'd gone, Ben and Zoe crawled out of their hiding place and approached the two elephants. They slung down their backpacks and knelt by them.

"We have to act quickly!" said Zoe.

Ben inspected the calf's injured leg. "This is horrible. There's so much swelling I can hardly see the snare." He began to cough. "And the infection stinks!"

As gently as he could, he tried to untie the wire. But Tomboi was not too weak to react. He stiffened and gave a bellow of pain.

Zoe stroked Tomboi's wrinkled head and cradled his limp trunk in her hands.

"We need sedation," said Ben. "Now!"

Zoe snapped into action. She wiped her eyes and pulled the tranquillizing gun and dart from her backpack. Ben stood up and aimed it into Tomboi's flank. Soon the little bull calf was unconscious.

There was a harsh cry above them. They looked up to see huge birds circling round.

"Vultures!" cried Zoe in alarm. She stood up and waved her arms angrily at them.

"The antibiotic in the solution is very strong so it should get to work soon," muttered Ben, as he worked on the bolas with a pair of pliers.

A loud trumpeting from along the track made the children leap to their feet. Through the trees they could see the herd of elephants approaching – the huge matriarch at their head.

"You hide, Zoe," said Ben. "I'll join you in a minute. Can't get this wire free…" His teeth were clenched and sweat was trickling down his face as he tried to get a grip on the bolas with the pliers.

"We're in this together," his sister replied. "I'll help." She raised Tomboi's limp foot. "Try round the other side."

Ben eased the point of the implement under the wire. "Got it!" he exclaimed.

There was a click and the snare sprang free from the little elephant's foot.

Zoe quickly threw their equipment into her backpack while Ben reloaded the tranquillizing gun with a second capsule and aimed it at Tomboi again.

"He'll be on his feet in a few minutes," he said, quickly retrieving both darts. "Erika told me this sedation reversal is super quick."

"And we'd better be super quick," said Zoe urgently. "Look!"

Ben glanced up. The huge matriarch was a few meters away now. Her eyes were wild with fear as she called anxiously to the two fallen members of her herd.

Ben and Zoe backed away to the safety of the trees as the herd surrounded Tomboi and his mother.

Some pressed forwards, feeling the cow all over with their trunks. Others paced round the group, rumbling sadly. Ben and Zoe could just see the matriarch curling her long trunk around Tomboi, who was struggling to get to his feet. With the help of two other cows, she lifted him up and supported him gently, holding him against her leg.

"Look out!" whispered Zoe. "I think they're on to us."

One of the largest elephants of the group was making its way towards them. Ben and Zoe cowered in fear as the huge grey beast towered above their hiding place. Then it raised its trunk, grasped the branch over their heads and tore it away. Others began to tear branches from the surrounding trees.

They laid them gently over the lifeless body of Tomboi's mother.

"It looks like a sort of funeral," whispered Ben in awe. "She must be dead."

Zoe watched, her tears falling silently.

The elephants stood silently round the
mound of leaves. The matriarch was the
first to move. She gently steered Tomboi
down the path with her trunk. The little
elephant gave one last pitiful look back,
and limped away with the herd.

CHAPTER ELEVEN

Ben took out his BUG and pressed the Wild hot key.

"I've managed to get an update from the Kenya Wildlife Service," came Uncle Stephen's voice. "They should be on their way soon."

"They're too late to save Tomboi's mother," said Ben. "She's been shot."

"And Tomboi?"

Ben told him everything that had happened. "The hunters are walking back to the lodge now," he finished.

"Well, they won't get far," Dr Fisher muttered. "I'll tip off the KWS and they can pick them up. I'll also make sure they get Zoe's video evidence – that way they'll have a cast-iron case against Hall and Chitundu."

Her eyes full of tears, Zoe walked over to say goodbye to Tomboi's mother. She bent down and gently removed the branches that covered her face. She stroked the lifeless forehead.

Then she started. Had one of the ears twitched? Frantically, she swept away the burial covering and put her hand on the elephant's side. The next second, she'd jumped to her feet.

"Ben!" she yelled. "Don't sign off. We've got to tell Uncle Stephen. Tomboi's mother is still alive!"

Two days later a small group of trekkers stood by the waterhole. It was a chilly morning and dawn had just broken, touching the tops of the trees with a golden glow.

Wambua turned to the tourists in his party. "Stand very still," he said, a big smile on his face. "Here come our beloved elephants."

Ben, Zoe and Erika watched eagerly as the pale-skinned matriarch led her herd down to the water on the opposite bank. Lester Hall stood slightly apart, snapping away at the scene.

"See the little calf?" Wambua went on. "Tomboi has just had a very lucky escape from hunters thanks to the Kenya Wildlife Service."

Ben and Zoe grinned at each other. No one could ever know Wild's part in the rescue, of course.

"Wambua sounds happy," said Ben, as the old man walked off. "No one's going to stop the Samburu protecting the elephants now."

"Tomboi's leg is healing nicely," Zoe whispered to her brother, as they watched the little elephant wading through some thick reeds, sticking close to Nyeupe. "I wish we could tell him his mother's alive and being looked after."

"And that those hunters won't be bothering them again," added Ben fervently.

"I'd love to have seen Mr Hall's face when they told him he wouldn't be hunting for a good long time," said Zoe gleefully.

"And Chitundu's sideline in bush meat is well and truly over," added Erika.

Frank Hall and Chitundu had been whisked away to the police station, each blaming the other, until they'd seen Zoe's video, which the police believed had been sent in by a tourist. Then they'd confessed everything.

It had been the talk of the lodge ever since. Runo had been very keen to tell the children about how Chitundu had gone mad since his arrest and kept rambling on about people spying on him from bushes. He'd also told them that his grandfather's elephant treks were on again and had asked – with a twinkle in his eye – whether Ben and Zoe would like to do the trip on a camel!

"I'm glad Lester's mum can't get out here for a few more days," said Ben. "He's cool – nothing like his dad."

"It'll be good to have him with us for the

rest of our stay," agreed Zoe.

Just then, Lester Hall came over to join them. He held out his camera to show his photos. "This is what I came to Africa for."

"They look great. You'll have loads to show your mum," said Zoe.

Lester looked serious for a moment. "Thanks for letting me hang out with you after ... what happened," he mumbled.

"It's OK," said Ben, giving him a friendly nudge. "See how well the calf is looking? You're a hero... I mean, that's what I heard. That you wouldn't let him be shot," he added quickly.

Lester went a bit pink at this.

Without thinking, Ben rubbed the plasters covering the ant bites and winced.

"What's that?" asked Lester.

"Ant bites," said Ben. He wondered what Lester would say if he knew how he'd got them!

Tomboi suddenly broke into a trot, sucked up a trunkful of water and blasted Nyeupe. The old matriarch splashed him back and he rolled over in the mud.

"That's one happy little elephant!" Zoe laughed.

WILD

AFRICAN ELEPHANT SURVIVAL

African elephants live in 37 countries of the African continent.

No. of African elephants living in the world today ⟶ 470,000-690,000
This is only 1% of the population noted in 1930.

Life span: up to 70 years
Oldest African elephant recorded: a male aged 82 years, which weighed about 12,000kg.

African elephants are the largest land animals on Earth and have the biggest ears in the world!

Male African elephants (bulls) can measure up to 4m in height and usually weigh over 6000kg – as much as 5 cars! Females (cows) can measure up to 2.8m in height and weigh about 3,600kg.

Females breed about once every two to four years. They are pregnant for 22 months – the longest pregnancy of any mammal. At birth, elephant calves weigh about 113kg and stand over 76cm tall. The calf relies on its mother's milk for up to 4 years.

STATUS: NEAR THREATENED

The African elephant is classified as "near threatened" on the red list of the International Union for Conservation of Nature. This means that if numbers decline it may be raised to threatened status.

RESCUE

AFRICAN ELEPHANT FACTS

THREATS

LOSS OF HABITAT

Loss of habitat is the biggest threat to the African elephant. In the whole of Africa less than 20% of the elephants' range is protected in parks and reserves. The elephants' territory is being reduced and broken up as people take it over and build roads and villages and grow crops. This can lead to conflict between elephants and villagers.

The trunk of an adult elephant is about 2 metres long and contains about 100,000 different muscles. It is used for smelling, breathing, trumpeting, digging, gathering food and sucking up water. African elephants have two finger-like features on the end of their trunk that they can use to grab small items, like berries or leaves. Elephants sometimes wrap their trunks together in displays of affection and greeting – a bit like a hug!

POACHING

Poaching for ivory from elephants' tusks used to be the main cause of the African elephant decline. International trade in ivory is now illegal, but poaching is still a threat. The WWF estimates that more than 12,000 elephants are needed each year to feed the demand for ivory.

It's not all bad news!

The World Wide Fund for Nature is working to improve the elephants' habitat and migration routes. In Kenya, the WWF is helping stop the conflicts between elephants and people and is finding ways of preventing elephants raiding crops. Special fencing has been developed that sends a warning text message to rangers when an elephant tries to break through it!

J. BURCHETT & S. VOGLER

WILD RESCUE

POLAR MELTDOWN

J. BURCHETT & S. VOGLER

WILD
RESCUE
AVALANCHE ALERT

Following reports that an unscrupulous marine park have dumped an unwanted young dolphin into the sea, Ben and Zoe are on their way to the Caribbean. Having been raised in captivity, the dolphin is ill-equipped for life in the open sea and soon finds itself in dangerous waters. It's up to Ben and Zoe to guide it to safety.

OUT IN JUNE 2010

J. BURCHETT & S. VOGLER

WILD
RESCUE
OCEAN S.O.S.

Following reports of a polar bear found dead near an Alaskan village, Uncle Stephen is sending Ben and Zoe to investigate. It is highly unusual for the animals to be found so close to human habitation. But the mission takes another turn when they learn that the dead bear had recently given birth. This means there are orphaned cubs out there. Will Ben and Zoe find them in time?

Ben and Zoe's skills are put to the test when they are dispatched to the treacherous slopes of the Himalayas. Following an avalanche, a mother snow leopard and her cub have been cut off from their territory and are surviving by eating sheep from a village. But now the angry locals are planning to protect their livestock by poisoning the leopards. It's down to the children to brave sub-zero temperatures and sheer rock faces, and protect the mother and her cub.

If you want to find
out more about
African elephants visit:

www.awf.org
www.wwf.org.uk
www.bornfree.org.uk